Natasha and the Bear

Illustrated by N.A. Ustinov

English adaptation by Paula Franklin

Silver Burdett Company
Morristown, N.J. and Agincourt, Ontario

Once upon a time in a village in Russia, a little girl named Natasha lived with her grandparents. One day some of her friends came by on their way to the woods to pick wild mushrooms.

"Oh, may I go with them?" asked Natasha.

"All right," answered her grandfather, "but don't become separated from your friends. You might get lost."

Natasha took a basket from her house and joined the other girls.

The woods were full of mushrooms because the weather had been rainy. Natasha stooped over and began cutting the soft white and brown delicacies from the forest floor. How happy her grandparents would be when she brought them home!

After a while, Natasha looked up. Her friends were gone, and she was all alone. "Where are you?" she called out. "Hello . . . hello . . ."

There was no answer, only the sounds of the forest.

Natasha didn't know what to do, so she started walking. She went deeper and deeper into the woods. But she couldn't find her friends. It began to get dark, and yellow-eyed owls hooted from the trees overhead. Suddenly Natasha saw a cabin in the mist. It was empty, so she went in.

Natasha had scarcely entered the log house when a huge bear appeared in the doorway.

"What are you doing in my house, little girl?"

Natasha was so afraid she couldn't speak.

"Well," said the bear, "you came at just the right time. I need somebody to work for me—you start tomorrow!"

The next morning, the bear set out for the woods carrying a basket in his paw. He called back to Natasha, "Don't try to run away while I'm gone. If you do, I'll catch you and eat you up!"

Many days passed. Natasha worked hard, carrying water, chopping wood, cleaning, and cooking for the bear. She was very homesick. She wanted to run away, but she knew she couldn't find her house. What could she do?

Then she had an idea.

"Mr. Bear," said Natasha, "I want to give a present to my grandparents. May I take it to the village?"

"No, you can't go," answered the bear, "but I'll take it for you."

Natasha's present was a great big bowl of delicious little cakes. After she had baked them, she pulled down a large basket from the shelf.

"Now, Mr. Bear," she said, "I'm putting the cakes in this basket. Please take it to Grandma and Grandpa. And don't eat any of the cakes on the way. I'll be watching you from the top of the oak tree."

As the bear grumbled that he would do what Natasha asked, she suddenly cocked her head to one side: "Is that rain I hear?" The bear went outside to see.

The bear looked up at the sky impatiently. "No, it's not raining. Is the basket ready?"

"I'm putting in the cakes," answered Natasha. And she climbed into the basket with the cakes on her head. When the bear came in, the girl was nowhere to be seen. He hoisted the basket onto his back and set off.

"This is really heavy," complained the bear as he sweated and strained over a hill. "And I'm hungry, too. She'll never notice if I eat a cake or two."

But as the bear slipped the basket off his shoulders, Natasha pretended to be calling from a distance. "No, no, Mr. Bear. I'm watching you from the top of the oak tree."

"What good eyesight that little girl has!" exclaimed the bear, embarrassed at being caught. He picked up the basket and trudged on.

Now the bear was really tired. He put down the basket and collapsed on a tree stump. But again he heard Natasha's voice calling, "No, no, Mr. Bear. I'm watching you. Keep going."

Suddenly four yapping dogs appeared and frightened the bear away. The dogs belonged to Natasha's grandparents. She was home!

The two old people came out of their house to find their beloved granddaughter climbing out of the basket. "Here I am," she said happily.

"Oh Natasha, we're so happy to see you again!" her grandparents cried out.

And they all lived happily ever after.

Adapted and published in the United States by
Silver Burdett Company, Morristown, N.J.
1985 printing
ISBN 0-382-09045-4
Library of Congress Catalog Card Number 84-40799
Depósito legal: M. 8503-1985
Edime, S. A. - Móstoles (Madrid)
Printed in Spain

About the Artist

Nikolai Ustinov was born at Ryazar in the Soviet Union. He studied art in Moscow at the Surikov Art Institute. He has contributed many humorous pictures and cartoons to newspapers. In the early 1960s he began illustrating children's books and has since made that his life's work.